THE GOOD EGG

To Alyssa, William, and Olive
—J.J.

For Allison
—P.O.

ISBN 978-1-338-60778-9

12 11 10 9 8 7 6 5 4   19 20 21 22 23 24

Printed in the U.S.A.   40

First Scholastic printing, November 2019

The artist used scanned watercolor textures and digital paint to create the illustrations for this book.

Typography by Jeanne Hogle

THE GOOD EGG

Jory John and Pete Oswald

SCHOLASTIC INC.

Oh, hello!
I was just rescuing this cat.
Know why?
Because I'm a good egg.

A *verrrrrrry* good egg.

It's true.
I do all kinds of good things. Like . . .

. . . I'll carry your groceries.

I'll water your plants.

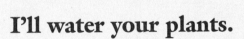

I'll change your tires.

I'll paint your house.

If you need any help whatsoever, I'm your egg.

I've *always* been a good egg. It's been this way from the start. Even in my earliest days . . .

. . . back at the store.

There were a dozen of us, living together under one recycled roof.

Fresh EGGS

There was Meg. And Peg. And Greg. And Clegg. And Shel. And Shelly. And Sheldon. And Shelby. And Egbert. And Frank. And *other* Frank.

The other eleven eggs weren't on their best behavior.
They weren't exactly . . . good.

They ignored
their bedtime.

They only ate
sugary cereal.

They threw tantrums.

**They cried for
no reason.**

They broke their stuff
. . . on purpose!

Meanwhile, I tried to take charge.
I tried to fix their bad behavior.
I tried to keep the peace.
Because I was a good egg.

A *verrrrrry* good egg.

Then, one fateful morning, I noticed some cracks in my shell.

They were *everywhere.*

My doctor said it was from all the pressure
I was putting on myself. The pressure of
making sure everybody was as good as me.

I was cracking up . . . *literally!*
Something *had* to change.
I'd had enough!

I told Meg and Peg and Greg and Clegg and Shel and Shelly and Sheldon and Shelby and Egbert and Frank and *other* Frank that I was leaving.

"I can't be the only good egg in a bad carton," I said. "Blah blah blah," they replied.

I left that night.

I wandered from town to town.

The hours became days.

The days became weeks.

I lost track of time.

I was alone.

Out there, on the road, under the stars, I really tried to focus on myself and what *I* needed.

I took walks.

I read books.

I floated in the river.

I wrote in my journal.

I found simple moments to be quiet.

I breathed in.

I breathed out.

I even started painting.

For once, I found time for *me*.

And guess what!

Little by little, the cracks in my shell started to heal.
My head no longer felt scrambled.

I started to feel like myself again.

So I've made a big decision.
I'm returning to my old carton and my friends.
Besides, I'm kind of lonely out here.

This time, I know what I need to do.

I'll try not to worry so much.

I'll be good to my fellow eggs while also being good to *myself*.

"Here we go. . . ."

Everybody missed me. I missed them, too.

"Hello, Meg. Howdy, Peg. Hey, Greg. Greetings, Clegg. What's up, Shel? Aloha, Shelly. Hey-o, Sheldon. Hi, Shelby. Good day, Egbert. What's happening, Frank? Howdy do, *other* Frank?"

Sure, every once in a while,
somebody's still a little bit bad.

But it's not like before.

Here's what I realized:
The other eggs aren't perfect,
and I don't have to be, either.

I'm OK with that.

Yep, the ol' carton is back together!
We're a solid dozen again.

It's good to be home.

Jory John is a *New York Times* bestselling author and two-time E. B. White Read Aloud Honor recipient. Jory's work includes the award-winning Goodnight Already! series; the bestselling Terrible Two series; the popular picture books *The Bad Seed*, *Penguin Problems*, and *Quit Calling Me a Monster!*; and the national bestseller *All My Friends Are Dead*, among other books. He lives in Oregon, where he buys eggs from his neighbor, who has chickens.

Pete Oswald is an LA-based artist, author, and illustrator. He's the cocreator of *Mingo the Flamingo*. Pete is also the illustrator of *The Bad Seed*, written by Jory John. When Pete isn't writing and illustrating books, he's working on numerous highly successful animated franchises as a character designer, concept artist, and production designer. He lives in Santa Monica, California, where he prefers his eggs fried, not scrambled.